Award winning author, Nicola May lives in Ascot in Berkshire. Her hobbies include watching films that involve a lot of swooning, crabbing in South Devon, eating flapjacks and enjoying a flutter on the horses.

Also by Nicola May

The Corner Shop in Cockleberry Bay
Love Me Tinder
The SW19 Club
Let Love Win
The School Gates
Better Together
Star Fish
Working it Out

For more information on Nicola May and her books, visit her website at www.nicolamay.com

CHRISTMAS SPIRIT

Nicola May

Nowell
Publishing

First published in Great Britain by Nowell Publishing 2013

Print Edition

You are not a human being in search of a spiritual experience. You are a spiritual being immersed in a human experience.

Teilhard de Chardin

PROLOGUE

'So you decide today of all days to tell me you are shagging that moth-eaten bag of fleas of a secretary of yours? How bloody clichéd.'

'I couldn't keep it in any longer.'

'Well, that's obvious!'

'The guilt was tearing me apart.'

'Oh, how my heart bleeds for you, Darren. I'm so pleased you have relieved yourself of that terrible burden – thanks for that.'

'It just... well, it just sort of happened.'

'How long has it been going on?' Evie's voice had taken on an animalistic growl. 'In fact, don't even answer that, I don't actually care.' She stormed towards the kitchen door and let out a tumultuous sneeze.

'Bless you.'

Evie swung around. 'Don't you fucking bless me, you conniving little shit.' She put on an affected voice. 'Oh, Evie, I really must stay over here, there, everywhere. Accounts to sort, juniors to fire. NO, Darren. Staff to UNDRESS more like!'

Tears were now streaming down her cheeks. 'Just fuck off, pack a bag and fuck off.'

Darren reappeared in the kitchen in what seemed like seconds with a large black suitcase on wheels.

'Oh, you'd already packed – silly me. As if you really would have thrown this one on me the day before Christmas Eve with no place to go. Not Darren Connors. He would always make sure number one was all right.'

Darren sighed and ran his hands through his blond floppy fringe.

'Evie, shit happens. There wasn't a day we weren't arguing lately. I think if we're honest, we both knew we were on borrowed time.

'Evie blew her nose loudly. 'But I never thought you'd be unfaithful,' she whispered, suddenly feeling too full of cold and too upset to fight.

'Oh, Evie.' Darren went to put his hand on her shoulder. 'Don't Evie me. Just go, Darren. I mean, what else is there to say, really?'

The lanky cleanshaven blond guy shrugged, picked his mail up from the side and shoved it in his pocket.

'So where are you going to live? 'Cos you're sure as hell not coming back here.' Evie sniffed loudly. 'Actually, don't answer that either. I really don't want to know.'

Darren guiltily bit his lip.

'How do you think I am going to be able to afford this place on my own?' Evie's voice had gone up an octave. 'I have just lost my bloody job – or had that slipped your tiny mind?'

'I'm sorry, Evie, I know the timing's not great, but you always fall on your feet – and anyway, I'm not your bloody meal ticket.'

Evie gasped, then remained open-mouthed as her boyfriend of two years carried on briskly, 'Look, I've left a month's rent in the pot, thought that'll give you time to sort yourself out. Get a lodger in maybe? I'll come and fetch the rest of my bits after Christmas.'

Overwhelmed with emotion, Evie's face contorted and she threw a massive fake smile. 'How very thoughtful of you, dear.' Then, gritting her teeth in anger, 'I hope Santa falls down the chimney and squashes you both to death.'

With that, she watched the man, formerly known as her lover, drag his cheating carcass and bulging case down the front path – and out of her life forever.

CHAPTER ONE

'Yes, I did say sherry.' Evie looked at the young barman in front of her and added impatiently. 'Blue bottle Bristol Cream if you've got it. With ice, yes, thanks.'

She raised her hand as she saw Bea approaching through the Christmas revellers. From the outside looking in, they were a strange pair. Bea, five foot ten, with gangly limbs and long dark shiny hair, and Evie, five foot four, with her blonde curls and curvy hour-glass figure.

They had become thick as thieves at a previous employ – mainly due to Evie nervously covering up Bea's scandalous relationship with the CEO of a rival company. Which (as most affairs do) ended in a sea of tears.

'You look like shit, Evie.'

Evie's blonde curls were more unruly than usual and her nose was red from blowing it.

'And good evening to you too, dear friend.' Evie managed a smile. 'It's this bloody cold. I need medicine.'

'Lucky they've got it here then.' Bea pointed to the sweet brown syrup sloshing around in her friend's glass.

'Anyone would think I was a freak, liking sherry.'

'Or maybe eighty-five.' Bea winked at the barman, who gave her a wry smile. She had always had a penchant for men much younger than herself. And Evie only wished she could have half the man-eating qualities as her friend.

They both laughed.

'Well, at least *you're* smiling,' Evie said to her friend.

'I can't believe the dick, to be honest.'

'Tell me about it, Bea. But the sad thing is, I wasn't surprised really.'

'Yeah, I know. It hasn't been a bed of roses, but I did think you'd work it through. How are you feeling after sleeping on it, anyway?'

'Hmm. Well, I cried when he told me last night, but I haven't cried since. If I'm true to myself I think I lost that loving feeling weeks ago. We were rarely having sex, and when we did I could tell his mind was elsewhere. I guess I didn't want to face the fact that I had another failed relationship on my hands.'

'Oh, Evie.'

'And I've literally got no money. Well, apart from a month's pay and the money Darren the

Dickhead left for me for rent. Most of which I intend to spend over Christmas to drown my sorrows.'

'I'm here for you, you know that.'

'I could always sell my camera.'

'You, my friend, are so *not* doing that. You know how much you love your photography – it keeps you sane. And there is work out there. In fact, I'm going to make sure we get you a new job *and* a new knob before January's out.'

Evie nearly spat her sherry out. 'What are you like? That is hilarious. But look at me: thirty-two and single on Christmas Eve. Unemployed and living in rented accommodation I can't afford. I mean, it can't get much worse, can it?'

'Oh, I'm sure it could.' A deep voice broke in between them.

'Sorry?' Bea made a questioning face at the stranger now in front of them.

'It could get worse if you wanted it to.'

The interloper was around six foot, in his early forties, had blue eyes with crinkly lines around them, a wide-mouthed smile, cropped dark hair and a small heart-shaped birthmark on his cheek. He noticed Evie staring at it.

'It has been more of a talking point rather than an avoidance point with the ladies, I've found.' His crinkly eyes were endearing and Evie felt herself turn as red as the Christmas lights flashing behind the bar.

'I... er...'

He laughed. 'I'm Greg and I'm slightly drunk, hence the bold interruption.'

'I'm Evie, also slightly drunk, and this is Bea, soon to be as drunk as the both of us. And what did you mean about it could get worse? I've just been jilted. I need my mood lightening, thanks.'

'Well, it could get worse because rather than be sat in a cosy house with plentiful alcohol and your roast turkey tomorrow, you could come and help me at the homeless shelter I manage. We're a man down.'

'And what makes you think that I'm such a saddo that I wouldn't have plans on Christmas Day?'

'These big flappy ears of mine, which couldn't help hearing about your tale of woe, that's what. But I'm not completely heartless: I am truly sorry to hear about your predicament.' He placed his hand on Evie's shoulder gently.

'Well unfortunately for you,' she said, 'I do have plans actually.' Bea took in Greg's handsome features and calm demeanour. He would be a perfect distraction for her pretty friend. And actually, she could tell already that Evie was quite taken with him.

'You don't any more, Evie. There's no room at my dining table from this very minute. My... er...

Auntie Flo's turkey has just escaped from the kitchen. She and Uncle Pete are having to come to me now.'

'Great!' Evie and Greg uttered in unison, with totally different connotations.

Evie downed her sherry and slammed her glass on to the bar. 'OK. OK. I'll do it.' She turned her head to the side and smiled up at the handsome stranger.

'You will?' Greg was buoyant.

'I've always thought about giving up my time on Christmas Day to help others less fortunate than myself.'

'Have you?' Bea screwed up her face.

'Yes, I have as a matter of fact, Beatrice Stewart. I just have always been too selfish to go through with it.'

'Well, that's marvellous, then.' Greg drained his glass. 'You can feel good about yourself too – and you need that sort of uplift at this moment, for sure.'

'Just tell me where and when I need to be. But wherever it is, I'm bringing a bottle of sherry.'

CHAPTER TWO

'Are you any good at stuffing?'

'Obviously not good enough or my boyfriend Darren wouldn't have run off with his secretary.'

Greg put his hands on his hips. His comic apron with a corkscrew hanging out from his crotch's position couldn't help but make Evie smile.

'I'm not saying sorry, because positive thoughts create positive happenings.'

'My boyfriend, or should I say ex-boyfriend, has just walked out on me. If you expect me to be a jovial Mrs Santa bloody Claus then you're barking down the wrong chimney, mister.'

'You're very beautiful when you're angry.' Greg laughed and placed a Christmas hat on her head.

Evie smirked and pulled her blonde curls out from under it.

'That's better. Now come on, Goldilocks, let's get these tables laid. We have many homeless bears to feed.'

By midday the other volunteers had all sprung into action and the Church Hall was full of Christmas Day hope. Paperchains hung from the ceiling, and children from a local primary school had created a huge sparkly mural which hung behind the food station. A huge Christmas tree in the corner was laden with donated tinsel and baubles, and a mass of presents awaited the homeless folks of East London. A hairdressing bay had been set up and even a chiropodist was giving his time up for the day. Evie was deeply touched by how many people were kind enough to give up their own special day to help others.

The buzz of the community spirit was overwhelming and it actually made her realise what a shallow existence she had been living with Darren. If she could have felt half the love she could feel around her now, she would without fail have been happy.

'I can't believe just how kind everyone is.' Evie placed the final gift out of the huge box that Greg had handed her. 'It's embarrassing to admit that I have never done anything so charitable in my whole life. To tell the truth, I don't even really like Christmas Day. All that fake joviality, usually ending in a hungover row about what to watch on television. I should have done this before.'

'Hmm. You might not ever want to do it again once we get to the end of the day.' Greg raised his eyebrows.

Evie looked him up and down. She usually liked men in their thirties, but at forty-two he was very handsome and she loved the little heart-shaped birthmark on his right cheek. She had a secret urge to kiss it.

She looked up at him and then quite spontaneously and naturally did so!

'Happy Christmas, Greg, and thank you so much.'

Greg put his hand to his cheek. 'Aw, that was nice, but thank you for what exactly?'

'Stopping me from moping about all day in complete misery. Aitchoo!'

'Bless you.' He took his hand away from his cheek and placed it gently under her chin.

'A pleasure,' he said. 'Right – let's make it a magical day for everyone, eh?'

'Yes, let's.' Evie smiled. 'Do you mind if I take some photos of the day?'

'No, of course not. That'd be great. In fact, if you don't mind we could use them for the website. Make it look fun, and it'll stop me from trawling bars to find last-minute waif and stray volunteers.'

'Oi!'

'Not that there is anything wrong with that, of course. I'm convinced it's the way forward.' He winked and went off to unlock the front door.

By 6 p.m. Evie's feet were killing her. She had never worked so hard in her life. Serving food, playing games, dishing out presents, chatting to everyone. She had had a misapprehension that homeless people might all be alcoholics or drug addicts – and to be honest had been slightly afraid. But so many of them had the saddest tales to tell and were genuinely lovely people. If you didn't have support of family and friends, she had learned how easy it was to fall into dire straits.

She was delighted at just how many poignant photos she had managed to take of the day, and couldn't wait to get home and pick out the best ones for the website.

Greg noticed her sit down quietly in the corner, take off her shoes and rub her feet.

'Hey. How's it going? I told you it would be hard work.'

'You weren't wrong, but I've loved it.'

'Good. Now head off if you like. The night shift will come on at eight but it's fine – we've got plenty of helpers if you really are knackered.'

'No bloody way! I'll be here until at least eight then, mister.'

'That's the spirit, Evie. I might even allow you

a quick sherry.'

Evie took a deep breath. This would be the perfect time to be bold and ask what she had been planning to ask for most of the day. Greg seemed such a good man, a million miles away from Duplicitous Darren. And he was really rather sexy too. He had smelled so delicious when she had kissed his cheek and she could just imagine how dreamy it would be to kiss those beautiful full lips of his. Even when he touched her shoulder she had felt a little spark of electricity.

If truth be told, she had wanted to split up with Darren months ago but because her job was insecure she had stupidly held on. And for what? Darren just wasn't worth it. She had simply been wasting time and she was determined not to miss her chance here. Too often in life she had held back and not said or done what she had thought was right at that moment in time.

Oh, to be more like Bea with her *Only regret the things you don't do* mantra. So it was with the thought of Bea's words of a new knob that she boldly sprang into action.

'So… um… Greg, what time are you here until then? I wondered if you…'

Just then, a petite elfin-featured girl, who must have been no older than twenty-five, ran full pelt at Greg and wrapped her legs around him.

'You made it.' He swung her around. 'Happy

Christmas, Shell.'

'Happy Christmas! The journey was a breeze actually.'

'Folks OK?'

'Good as gold, I have presents in the car for you from them.'

Evie felt her heart sink. She has known this man for only a few hours, but already could already feel his warmth and kindness. She had even felt that there could be a connection between them.

'Evie, Michelle, Michelle, Evie.'

'Lovely to meet you, Evie.' The girl jumped down and shook her hand lightly. 'Saint Greg here said he had managed to rope another unsuspecting helper in. I'm on the night-shift, for my sins.'

Evie smiled. You couldn't help but like this bubbly girl too, with her joy and effervescence of life. She could see why Greg was with her. Suddenly, without warning, tears pricked her eyes. 'Right, best get clearing up that wrapping paper,' she said chokily and shot off to the other end of the hall and through the door there.

An ambulance whizzed by, blue lights a-flashing as she sat on the steps of the church hall, and she felt sad for the poor person in trouble today of all days. She took deep breaths to compose herself, then shivered as the December evening air engulfed her coatless body.

Tears began to run down her cheeks. 'What a

bloody mess,' she said out loud.

'Here.' A heavy, slightly musky-smelling coat was put over her shoulders as a man joined her on the steps and lit an equally musky-smelling pipe. 'There is a solution to everything in this life apart from death, you know.'

Evie reached for a tissue in her apron and blew her nose loudly. She couldn't speak for tears, so without looking up she nodded as the man continued.

'So, let me guess: the big drama is that the tall man with the Santa hat and the heart-shaped birthmark is in love with someone other than you – correct?' Evie could detect a posh accent. 'I'm Yves by the way, Yves with a Y.'

'Evie – Evie with an E.' She wiped her eyes and turned to face her step companion.

'Ah, she speaks with humour, as well as weeps.'

'Yves and Evie. Ha! That's quite a coincidence.'

'Nothing in this world is a coincidence, Evie with an E, eh? Hmmm. My mum was French, my birthday was yesterday, my dad had a sense of humour – go figure.'

'That's brilliant. I recognise you now – I dished up your carrots earlier.'

'And you did it so finely too. *That woman with the blonde wig*, I thought to myself. *She sure knows how to dish up veg*.

Evie couldn't help but smile. 'You cheeky bastard. And as for your wig insinuation, no one in their right mind would want to pay good money for this unruly mop.'

'That's better. The frown has been turned upside down.'

'Aw, I like that!'

'And your curls make you who you are, so stop all that vocal self-harming right this minute. I suppose you don't like your curves either?' Yves went on. 'Want to look like the skinny kid that had her arms wrapped around Greg, I bet?'

Evie loving his frankness, nodded.

'Well, embrace those curves too, honey, as I say they just make more of you to love.'

'You must think me such a trivial bitch. My problems are nothing compared to yours.'

'And there I expect you are very wrong, lady. Go on, tell me why you are sad? I'm a good listener and I've got plenty of time on my hands.'

Evie noticed Yves's green eyes. They still had a wonderful sparkle despite him living on the street. He had a full beard that was actually not too badly kept, and his skin was remarkably clear and not as weather-beaten compared to other people's were that she had spoken to today. His jumper and jeans were worn but clean, and he actually smelled quite fresh. His right boot was tied round with string to keep the sole on and he wore a silver earring in the shape of a dove in his right ear.

As if he could read her mind, he took her hand gently. She could feel his rough palm. 'I stayed in a hostel last night,' he told her. 'Washed, brushed up, and one of the helpers gave me a new pair of undies and a squirt of his aftershave. I mean, I didn't know who I might meet today, did I?' His teeth were slightly stained, from his pipe-smoking, she assumed.

'You don't look old enough to be smoking a pipe,' she commented.

'All these preconceptions the real world conforms to. Age is purely a number, it shouldn't be a label for anything.' He scratched his beard. 'I suck on the pipe more out of habit than anything. It's quite enjoyable. If I score baccy it's a bonus – wanna try?'

'No, you're all right, thanks. So what about you? I'm interested to hear your story.'

'I asked you first. Come on, humour me a little, Evie. I mean, my entertainment tonight isn't going to involve catching up on the soaps or a *Gavin & Stacey* Christmas special, now is it?'

'I so feel for you.'

'Don't. Now speak.'

Evie pulled her knees in under the old grey overcoat. 'Well, I really like Greg, but he's not the reason for my tears.'

'Go on.'

'Are you sure you want my tales of woe?'

'Evie, talk!'

'OK. OK. My boyfriend dumped me two days ago. He's fucking his secretary. I lost my job two weeks ago. I'm thirty-two and have a body clock ticking as loudly as Big Ben and I can't afford to stay in my rented house unless I get a lodger. And I really don't fancy sharing with a stranger.' She was on a roll now. 'I knew things weren't right with me and Darren. He was pretty selfish, a real mummy's boy, never did any chores. Always knew his parents would bail him out. He had the sex drive of an amoeba anyway, so in fact good bloody riddance to him, I say. Aitchoo!'

'Bless you.'

'Thank you.'

'And as for Greg, well, I met him two nights ago in a pub in Chelsea and he randomly asked if I would help here today. He's the first man who's shown me an inch of kindness for a while and he is rather hot.'

Yves sucked on his pipe and shivered slightly.

'Do you want your coat back?'

'No, it's fine. I'm used to the cold.'

A couple walked by hand in hand, laughing, then stopped and kissed right in front of them.

'Happy Christmas!' they both shouted back in unison as they ran towards a black cab.

'So, out of all those things you said that were making you sad, which one of them doesn't have a solution?'

Evie looked up to the starry sky in thought.

'There's going to be a frost,' she noted.

'Evie, I asked you a question.'

'Well, none of them, I suppose. In time I will get a job and a house. I need a man to get a baby, and that's what I always struggle with. Finding a decent man. I've got a worse track record than Elizabeth Taylor, as a matter of fact.'

'See, it's not so bad – and who says you need a man to get a baby these days?'

'True.'

'And wouldn't you rather have had the colourful life that Elizabeth Taylor led, than be someone for example who stayed in a loveless marriage for the security of it?'

'Well, if you put it like that... I can't believe I'm being so candid but if I'm totally honest, I am materialistic. I don't like not having money or love in my life for that matter. I don't want to have to scrape to buy a lipstick or treat a magazine as a luxury item. I'm too old to be living like a student again.'

'Thar she blows again about age.' Yves sucked harder on his pipe.

'I mean, what sort of quality of life can you have without money, Yves? I hate to say it, but you are a prime example. You have one good boot, your clothes are horrible, you don't have a bed to sleep in. I don't believe you can ever wake up feeling happy.'

Yves ignored her comment and offered Evie his hand to help her up. She sneezed again loudly. He took his coat gently from her shoulders, reached into a pocket and dabbed a menthol-smelling yellow cream under her nose.

'Oi.' She pulled away. 'What do you think you're doing?'

'Trust me and meet me five p.m. tomorrow on the steps of St Paul's Cathedral.'

Evie finished wiping her nose and turned to answer, but the young tramp had already disappeared into the cold December night.

CHAPTER THREE

'What do you mean, someone put some ointment under your nose and your cold has completely gone?'

'Just that. Honestly, it was the weirdest thing. I'm no longer sneezing, my sore throat's gone, even the cough. I'm one hundred per cent better; in fact, I feel bloody great.'

'It's just a coincidence, Evie. I mean, colds do that. They come and then they go.'

'He told me there was no such thing as a coincidence.'

'Who is this man who has brainwashed you, anyway?'

'His name's Yves. He was born on Christmas Eve so his parents called him Yves. He's a tramp.'

'I know it's only ten o'clock but are you on the sherry already?'

'No. I'm not! I met him at the homeless shelter. He's sweet. He said some lovely things. I'm meeting him later actually. At St Paul's.'

'I think you've gone mad – and where does the

lovely Greg feature in all this?'

'The lovely Greg has a girlfriend, unfortunately. I was all set to ask him out for a drink and she suddenly appeared. All petite and perfect, to work the night-shift with him.'

'Well, it's just a girlfriend, not a wife. You 're still in with a chance if you play your cards right.'

'Bea, you are terrible! I do have some morals. Anyway, Happy Boxing Day you old tart. How was yesterday?'

'Just the usual. Mum, Dad and the sisters. Auntie Flo, Uncle Pete. Oh, and Tom and Vera came round from next door with number one son, Josh, for the evening.'

'And did you?'

'Just a blow job, in the utility room.'

'You are unbelievable.'

'He's twenty-four now. He'll be too old for me soon.'

'I wish I had your gall.'

'It's short-lived gratification, Evie, and it's not big or clever. Just a complete and utter turn-on.'

'Don't ever change, Beatrice Stewart.'

'So, back to Yves the tramp. I can't believe I'm even having this conversation. Why are you meeting him later?'

'I don't actually know.'

'What?'

'Well, there's something about him. He is really

interesting. I feel drawn to him.'

'Come on down! Meet Beatrice Stewart, shagger of toy boys and her friend Evie Harris with her fetish for tramps.'

Evie laughed out loud. 'Let me just go with it.'

'He might be after your money.'

'What bloody money? Nah, he knows I'm skint.'

'OK. Well, be careful and make sure you call me later and give me the scoop.'

'I will. What are you doing later anyway?'

'Hopefully, Josh. His mum and dad are going out and I said I'd pop round to pull his cracker later.'

'You are insatiable, girl.'

'I know! Now, bugger off and go and see old Christmas Yves, you weird tart.'

'He's not old.'

'You said he was a tramp?'

'Look at you labelling. It's hard to tell exactly how old he is, as he has a bushy beard and a few laughter lines, but he's only around thirty, I reckon.'

'Get in there then, girl. Who knows? This could be the man of your dreams.'

'You make my heart smile, Bea. You really do.'

'Good. Enjoy yourself whatever you do and I cannot wait to hear all about it.'

CHAPTER FOUR

Peace

It was eerily quiet on the tube on Boxing Day and Evie enjoyed the tranquility. One benefit of being out of work, she thought, was that she could step out of the rat race, even if just for a short while.

Yves was wearing a light grey suit and his beard looked slightly shorter than she remembered. He was waiting at the bottom of the steps to the spectacular St Paul's Cathedral. Evie had read about the cathedral on her iPhone on the way here. *She could recite off pat the fact that it sits at the top of Ludgate Hill, the highest point in the City of London, is dedicated to Paul the Apostle and dates back to the original church on this site, founded in AD something or other. The present church had been designed by Sir Christopher Wren. Phew!*

Despite the area around the cathedral being well lit, Yves shone a torch towards her so Evie's path was even clearer. Today, his brown hair was tied back in a short ponytail. She hated to admit it but he did look quite handsome in a hippyish sort of way.

'Hello Evie with an E, how are you?'

'My cold has gone! I feel so much better. Haven't sneezed even once today.'

'I'm glad to hear it.'

'What *was* that ointment you put under my nose? Is it a wonder cure?'

'Ointment? Sorry, I don't understand. I had some hand cream on that they had put in the toilets yesterday, maybe it was that you smelled?'

'Oh, maybe.' Bea was right, she was imagining things. Her cold had gone, and for this she was pleased – whatever the reason.

'These are for you.' She handed Yves a carrier bag.

'Trainers? Wow. That's really kind. Thank you – and they're the right size.'

'Well, I thought you looked about the same build as Darren, and he won't miss them. He's got hundreds of pairs.'

'I really appreciate that, Evie. Right, I'm glad you are early. Evensong is about to start and I want you to experience it.'

Evie wasn't particularly religious; she had gone to a Church of England school and that was about as far as it went. She knew the Lord's Prayer and a few hymns, was all.

However, she gasped as she entered the cathedral. She had obviously seen it on the television at various state occasions and had seen images of Charles and Diana getting married there.

'Was Diana's funeral here too?' She was whispering now.

'No, Westminster Abbey.' Yves tucked his pipe in his pocket.

Evie giggled. 'We should go up to the Whispering Gallery.'

'Ssh. Another day.' Yves' beard tickled her ear.

They were ushered to seats right within the choir stalls. Once everyone was settled, it was the loudest silence she had ever experienced. The beauty of this magnificent place of worship overtook her and her eyes filled with tears. Yves reached for her hand and squeezed it. She was in awe of the magnificently painted ceiling, the ornate gold decorations, the architecture, the sheer size of the place.

But, most of all she was overcome by the sudden feeling of peace that washed over her when the choir began to sing. She took a deep breath and thought of her beautiful mum, as she always did when she ventured into a church. Celia Harris had died when she was just thirty-five, of a sudden brain haemorrhage, and it had been the single most horrific event to date in Evie's whole life. She was so glad that Celia had had her when she was just seventeen, as it had at least given her eighteen glorious years with her mother. She still missed her every single day. Celia had not only been an amazing person, but also a gifted artist, and Evie knew that if she had been allowed to reach her potential, her paintings would have made it to top London galleries. Such a waste of a beautiful life.

Evie knew her love of photography must have come from her creative mother. She had never met the man who had fathered her. She was the much-loved result of a dubious one-night stand, Celia had told her, and nothing more glamorous than that. Evie wasn't angry: she had loved the frankness and eccentricity of her adored mother, and didn't miss having a father in her life.

Evie had read somewhere that love and peace are supposed to fill the hole that a bereavement brings. She was yet to experience that, but hoped one day it might come true.

The last hymn reached its heartwarming crescendo and Yves guided her out of the choir stalls and towards the Nativity Scene, which had been set up on the way out of the cathedral.

'It's so sweet,' Evie said quietly.

She then noticed rows and rows of lit tea-lights. They looked so beautiful and it felt so Christmassy. Without prompting, she put her money in the box for one. Wishing her mum happiness wherever she might be, she lit it, put it amongst the others. Quietly at first, then more loudly on reaching the cold fresh air, she began to sob. Big, fat, snotty sobs on to Yves shoulder.

He rubbed her back gently. 'It's OK, Evie, get it out. You will feel so much better.'

After about five minutes she stopped and pulled away from him.

'I am so sorry.'

'Never ever apologise for expressing emotion, Evie. And if anyone is not kind enough to comfort or understand you when you do, then they are not worthy of your time or love.'

'Thank you.' She blew her nose.

'Can I ask who it was?'

'My mum.'

Yves shut his eyes. 'I feel your pain and bless you.' After a moment, he went on: 'When you asked about Diana's funeral earlier, I remembered her sister reading the most beautiful piece.'

'Go on, will it make me cry again though?'

'Maybe, but it is so beautiful. I want to share it with you.'

They walked down the cathedral steps together, an unlikely couple, but Evie didn't mind what anyone thought. Yves had such a good soul – who cared if he looked a bit of a mess. It really didn't matter. Without warning he started to recite –

Time is too slow for those who wait,
Too swift for those who fear,
Too long for those who grieve,

Too short for those who rejoice,
But for those who love, time is eternity.

All of a sudden, some fireworks lit up the night sky behind the dome of the cathedral.

'I adore fireworks.' Evie laughed happily. 'How magical is this. Who wrote that poem, by the way?'

'It was a guy called Henry van Dyke, a nineteenth-century American author, educator, and clergyman.'

'You're far too clever to be a tramp.'

'Another unfounded generalisation, Evie with an E. Now what was it that the dandy Oscar Wilde said? *One has a right to judge a man by the effect he has over his friends*. But I won't bore you with more of my quotations.'

'You've haven't bored me once. Thank you from the bottom of my heart for bringing me here. It's been truly amazing and I feel honoured that I could get upset in front of you.'

'See, you don't need money to do things that make you feel good.'

'No, tonight does prove that, but please let me get you dinner to say thank you?'

'Evie, if you were to use one word to describe to me how tonight's experiences have made you feel – the singing, the surroundings, the candle, your release of tears – what would it be?'

Without hesitation, Evie replied very softly,

'Peaceful. Yes – peaceful, that's how I feel.' She smiled at him. 'So, dinner?'

Yves shook his head, placed a piece of white card in her hand, closed her fingers around it and was gone.

The small, business-sized card had the most beautiful water-colour painting of a dove on one side, and on the other in perfect handwriting were the words: *Meet me at the bottom of The Shard tomorrow night, half an hour before sunset.*

CHAPTER FIVE

'He obviously wants to shag you.' Bea put a glass of white wine down in front of her friend and sat back in a leather sofa in their favourite Chelsea bar.

'Oh Bea, not everyone thinks at such a base level as you,' Evie said, then looked around the place. 'Quiet in here today, isn't it?'

'Yes, I guess everyone's saving themselves for New Year's Eve.'

'I hate this mid-Christmas lull time. It's so quiet at home without Darren too. But weirdly, I don't miss *him*, just the company, I suppose. I was usually in the bedroom whilst he watched sport in the lounge anyway.'

'I know you said definitely no before, but maybe it is a good idea to get somebody to share with you. You need to get someone to split the rent or you'll have to get out anyway.'

'Yes, I know – but I don't even want to think about it now. I'm all right up until the end of January, then I'll be homeless too.'

'Well, that's all right, you can snuggle down underneath the arches with your new mate. Where does he sleep anyway?'

'We haven't talked about it.'

'Really? I'd be interested to know. God, I bet his cock smells rank.'

'Bea! Being friends with you is like being friends with a man, you are so bloody coarse. And anyway, he doesn't seem to smell that bad actually. I think he must be staying at a hostel where he can wash and store the stuff he has got. I will ask him just for you later.'

'Later? You're seeing him again!'

'Um, yeah.'

'You haven't really told me much about last night either, just you went to St Paul's Cathedral, saw a choir, lit a candle and he disappeared again.'

It had been such a special experience that Evie felt she wanted to keep it to herself. Bea belittling it would take some of the magic away. And it had been really special. In fact, she was really looking forward to seeing Yves later. She felt drawn to him in a way she couldn't explain.

'I'm starving but I'm going to wait to eat until I get home, I can't spunk any more of the rent money on food, can I?'

'I'll treat you, Evie – it's fine, darling. You know my City bonuses are disgustingly massive.'

'Well, as long as you're sure. And you know as

soon as I get a job I'll repay the favour.'

'Evie, you are one of the most generous friends I have. Please just let me treat you without even thinking like that. It's a Christmas present, OK?'

'OK, but I can't drink much. I'm meeting Yves at the bottom of The Shard – and if we are going up there, I shouldn't really get drunk.'

'With your fear of heights, honey, I think you *should* have a drink. And anyway, I think it costs a fair bit to go up there, so I doubt if that's what you'll be doing.' Bea chuckled. 'I've been waiting on an invite to go up there. Mind you, it will be a brave man who asks if I want to be taken up The Shard, without repercussions.'

Evie's face remained deadpan. 'Bea, you will never go to heaven.'

'As if I'd bloody want to. I mean, nobody who's any fun will be there for me to play with.'

CHAPTER SIX

Freedom

Evie snapped her laptop shut. She had no idea what time it would get dark tonight and thought she had better check. She didn't want to be hanging around at the bottom of The Shard waiting in the cold. She was glad she had decided on just the one glass of wine with Bea as she had no wish to travel across London feeling tipsy. With an hour to kill, she walked to the kitchen to flick on the kettle. As she did so, her mobile rang.

'Evie, hiya – it's Greg.'

She felt her heart lift a little.

'I don't know what happened yesterday,' he went on. 'I got tied up with Shell and then I couldn't find you. I just wanted to say thanks SO much for all your help. You did a great job and loads of people sang your praises, including some of the homeless boys – and that doesn't happen often, you know.'

'Aw, that's nice. Thanks for letting me know.

Yeah, sorry, I… being honest, Greg, I got a bit upset and felt I had to go home.'

'Oh no. You should have come to me. We all need a hug sometimes and evidently I'm rather good at them.'

Evie went silent. The thought of being embraced by the big, handsome, kind Greg needed a moment of contemplation.

'Anyway, I was wondering if you might be free another day this week as the Centre is open throughout the Christmas period and I always need some extra hands?'

'Yes, yes of course. I can come tomorrow if you like and let's go from there.'

'Perfect. Don't rush in – turn up, say, eleven at the same Bethnal Green site.'

'No problem. See you then – and thanks, Greg.'

'It's you that's helping me. See you tomorrow.'

He hung up and Evie looked at her handset to check if the call had closed properly. Staring back at her was the screensaver of her and Darren. They had got a passer-by to take it on a long weekend to Amsterdam when they had first met. Love's young dream, so many plans, hopes and dreams. She started to cry. Yes, he had been a bastard, but two years was a long time to spend with anyone and they had had their good times. He hadn't even sent a *Happy Christmas* message – but then why would he? He was now ensconced in the cheating arms of

Anna McShea, ten years his junior and a bitch! Evie knew she should really delete his number, but letting go had never been a speciality of hers.

Puffing her cheeks out, she exhaled noisily. '*Onwards and upwards*' was what her dear mum always used to say, and that was exactly what she would do. She would just have to get on and make the best of it.

Yves waved and smiled as Evie reached the bottom of The Shard. *(This is an iconic, landmark building on the London skyline, designed by master architect Renzo Piano. At a height of 310m one of the tallest buildings in Western Europe, The Shard redefines London's skyline and will be a dynamic symbol of the capital, recognisable throughout the world.)*

When she reached him, he emptied his pipe and tucked it in the pocket of the heavy overcoat he had been wearing on Christmas Day.

She looked up at the magnificent building and felt slightly sick at the thought of even going halfway up it. She hoped that Bea was right and that it would be too expensive for a homeless man and unemployed woman to undertake.

'Hello.' She greeted him with a wide smile. 'These are for you.' She handed him a small box of fine truffles. 'These were a gift. I've eaten one but thought you might like the rest?'

'That's kind. Thanks, Evie. How you doing?'

'I'm fine, Yves. I had such an amazing time at St Paul's. What a beautiful and peaceful place.'

'Good. I hope that today will be just as memorable. Now follow me, quickly please.' Yves pulled her into a doorway, where they were faced with another homeless man who had set up camp there. 'Ralph,' he asked, 'did you sort it?'

'Yeah, man. Down there.' He pointed to a large carrier bag at his feet.

Evie could smell his rancid breath and turned her head away. 'Here, thanks mate.' Yves handed him the chocolates and his old boots that had now been replaced by Darren's shiny trainers. He grabbed the carrier bag and Evie followed him to yet another doorway, where he tipped the contents of the bag on the floor.

'Perfect. Put these on, Evie, we are going on a little ride.'

'I can't do this, Yves, I just can't.' Evie had never felt so sick.

'Never say or think of negatives, Evie. Positivity breeds positivity.'

'That's what Greg says.'

'And Greg is right. Now embrace this experience, it's going to be amazing.'

'What if we get arrested?'

'We won't, I promise you. Ralph is going to deter security, and also thanks to him we have hard hats and safety harnesses for extra safety – and of course to stop immediate suspicion.'

Evie shook her head in disbelief, not believing just how much trust she was putting in this nigh-on stranger.

'If we fall one thousand feet, a hard hat will of course save our lives,' Evie said flippantly. 'Oh Lord, are you sure you know how to work this thing?'

'Evie, stop it!'

Her eyes were closed tightly. 'Tell me when it's all over.'

'Onwards and upwards!' Yves shrieked as he pressed a button and the window-cleaning cage started to lurch upwards.

It seemed like an eternity before the cage came to a stop. Evie's eyes were still closed tight and Yves had to smile at her pretty face and the wafts of curls that were coming out of her hard hat.

'Right, sit down slowly: you will feel safer then.'

He faced her, wrapped his legs around her and held both her hands tightly. The cage was made of glass. The cold wind whipped around their heads but the structure was steady, so the cage remained static.

'Now open your eyes.'

'Fuck! Fuckety fuck fuck fuck. I want to die.'

'Take a huge deep breath from your tummy, Evie, remove the fear from your mind and look around you.'

Evie breathed deeply, sending plumes of icy smoke into the air. She was too scared to move a single inch.

'Don't look down, just across. You are very safe. You are just frightened of fear itself.'

Evie did as she was told and then opened her mouth in pure amazement. The sky was on fire with the most beautiful sunset she had ever seen. Every single landmark she had visited or seen in the media was in front of her eyes. She could see the Thames winding its watery journey to the sea. It was the most magnificent view she had ever seen.

'I should have brought my camera,' she breathed. 'To capture this, would be heavenly. I know what birds must feel like now.'

'You don't need photos, like you don't need money to enjoy the most wonderful experiences. Just live in this present moment, Evie. Etch this view in your mind, and whenever you are feeling sad and low, bring it to the fore and remember its magnificence.'

Evie, without warning, started to cry.

'What's wrong?' Yves squeezed her hands tightly.

'I was with Darren for two years, and in two days I have shared moments with you like I have never shared with anyone before.'

'Let him go, Evie, let him go with love. We should all let go of the negative people in our lives as they do not help us move forward. If someone has hurt you in the past, you don't have to forgive them to their face, but in your heart. Thank them for the experience they gave you and let it go. Remind yourself that you had to go through it for your own spiritual growth.'

'I think you are right. So many people do drain my energy and I guess there are some people you can only help so much before they can help themselves.'

'Exactly. And letting go of anger and resentment from unwanted past experiences will allow loving and healthy new experiences to come into your life. As I said before, be grateful for what you have in the present moment.'

'You're really quite special, aren't you, Yves.' She paused. 'And I don't even know your surname?'

'Look at Tower Bridge opening up,' was all he replied.

'Wow! All the years I've lived in London and I have never seen that happen before.' Evie was so thrilled.

'Do you think you can stand up now?'

'Yes, hold me though. This is SO scary.'

'You need to see just one more thing.'

Evie held Yves's arm tightly as he helped her up. She checked that her harness was locked on, and grasped the side of the cage with her other hand.

'Oh, my! Oh, Yves.'

Darkness had fallen and slowly but surely lights began to come on and twinkle across the beautiful capital city of London. Headlights, street lights, Christmas lights, house lights. It really was the most spectacular sight she had ever seen.

'This is an unbelievable experience. Thank you so much.' She moved her hand from the side of the cage and stroked his cheek.

'Right, Evie with an E, you have one thing left to do up here. It will involve you letting go of me and the cage but literally for seconds.'

'OK.' Evie couldn't even imagine what it could possibly be, but she was so 'in the moment' she didn't care what it was.

'An old Reiki teacher of mine taught me this and it definitely works in freeing your emotions.'

'Go on.'

'I'm allowing you – just briefly, mind – to think of situations and people who have caused negativity in your life. All you have to do is pretend you are holding an imaginary axe, then bring it down really hard as if you are chopping a massive piece of wood and shout NO at the top of your voice as you do so.'

Evie screwed up her face. 'That's a bit weird. I'm not sure.' She was beginning to really feel the cold now too. 'I want to go down,' she said in a babyish voice.

'Do it, Evie – I know it will help you. And there is no better place to do it than here. Only me, the birds and the angels will hear you. Then we will go straight down and get warm. I promise.'

Suddenly, without hesitation, Evie lifted the imaginary axe and chopped the wood as hard as her little arms would allow her.

'NO! NO! NO!'

'There's a girl, Evie. Now come on, let's get you down now.'

'I insist I treat you to a hot drink after that, at least.' Evie was immensely relieved to reach terra firma.

Yves shook his head. 'If you were to use one word to me to describe how tonight's experiences have made you feel, what would it be?'

'Free. Yes, free.' Yves just nodded wisely as Evie continued. 'That was a truly astonishing experience. I wonder what old Henry van Dyke would say about *that*?'

'He'd probably say "less of the old".'

Evie laughed. 'Now, how about that drink?'

Yves placed a white postcard in her hand and before she had a chance to say anything else, he was gone.

She read one side and felt moved.

If All the Skies

If all the skies were sunshine,
Our faces would be fain
To feel once more upon them
The cooling splash of rain.

If all the world were music,
Our hearts would often long
For one sweet strain of silence,
To break the endless song.

If life were always merry,
Our souls would seek relief,
And rest from weary laughter
In the quiet arms of grief.

She turned over to be greeted by a magnificent water-colour painting of an eagle and the words: *Meet me outside Shakespeare's Globe, Thursday at* 2.

CHAPTER SEVEN

'Well, I reckon it all sounds a bit weird. I mean, wouldn't you rather be screaming YES! YES! YES!?' Bea had insisted on a coffee and cake catch-up in her local cafe.

'Weird it may be, but I am suddenly feeling a whole lot better about things. Lighter, almost. I can't explain.'

'I can't believe that you, one – didn't get one arrested, or two – pooh yourself doing what you both did. Complete madness in my eyes.'

'Ew. I was just about to order a brownie but I think I'll have a flapjack instead. You are so vile sometimes. Talking of which, did young Josh take you up "The Shard"?'

'Who's being vile now?'

'No, he's a bit inexperienced really. Feels like he's digging for gold rather than my G spot. Undoubtedly, all these young guys' bodies and the thrill of forbidden fruits gives me a buzz, but to be honest I really am ready for a real man.'

'Blimey, have you got a temperature?'

'No, honestly Evie – I need to sort myself out. Stop playing games, pretending I don't want to commit. I want to settle down and have a family as much as you do really.'

'Wow. Beatrice Stewart. Although, I have heard this before.' They both laughed.

'You never know though, maybe your new-found weirdo goodness is rubbing off on me, eh?'

'It's not really that weird, and anyway I need to get a move on as I'm due at the homeless shelter with Greg again at eleven.'

'I'm really pleased you are doing stuff and not moping around.'

'This poem helped.' Evie handed Bea the post-card with the van Dyke poem, and could see her eyes water.

'Oh my God, that is just so beautiful and so true. Do we really always want sunshine, flowers and music 24/7? No! We wouldn't appreciate them then. That Henry fella knew what he was talking about.'

Evie laughed. 'Didn't he just. Right, let me stuff this flapjack down and then I'd best go and put on something decent. Who knows, Gorgeous Greg might have realised that he doesn't want an elfin nymphet and that a voluptuous blonde is his calling, after all.'

'Before you go, what about New Year's Eve? *Alfie's* are having a ticket only black-tie event or the Heart and Flowers have got a live band, everyone welcome.'

'Budget says Heart and Flowers, if you don't mind?'

'OK. Let's do it, it will be packed and fun. We'll talk later re. arrangements.'

Greg's face lit up as he saw Evie through the glass door and ran to unlock it. The Centre appeared empty.

Despite being ten years her senior he really was attractive and she undeniably fancied him. Yves kept telling her off about harping on about age and it being just a number. Maybe his lessons were actually beginning to kick in.

'Hello. Good to see you, Evie.' He kissed her on the cheek and she felt a little electric shock in her legs. She had noticed that since she had opened up about her mum and let go of negativity, that she was getting these shock-type feelings a lot more. Earlier, when a song she liked came on the radio, she had experienced it. It felt odd, but rather lovely all at the same time.

'No Shell today then?'

'No, she's gone back up North – she's in her last year at med school. I hardly see her at the moment, which is a shame.'

'Sorry to hear that.' Was she? Was she really sorry? No, if she was honest with herself, of course she wasn't. She would never try to come between a couple, but what if Greg decided to kiss her passionately and offered a 'lewd interlude' in the store cupboard? Could she resist? Hmm, maybe not. She noticed how good his bum looked in his jeans today and recalled that she hadn't had sex for at least two months.

'Evie, Evie!' Greg shouted across the hall.

'Sorry, miles away.'

'Would you mind getting the food out of the ovens? It's all easy stuff today as we are short of volunteers.'

'Of course not. I'm here to do whatever you need me to do.'

They worked in unison to set the food ports up.

'How are you feeling now anyway?' Greg asked. 'You said you were upset on Christmas Day.'

'So much better actually. I met one of the homeless guys outside as I was leaving. He is an extraordinary character and has made me feel more at ease with the situation, to be honest.'

'Well, that's good. Is it the break-up that's upsetting you?'

She didn't dare tell him she had had a mad moment of jealousy about his girlfriend.

'I guess, plus my lack of a job and my wanting

a family.'

'Oh Evie, it will all come good. I feel the same about a family too. But I'd rather wait until I'm with the right person than do it as a knee-jerk reaction.'

Before Evie could ask if Shell was the right person, there was a loud banging on the door as the first of the hungry appeared.

She looked out for Yves, but he didn't come and she felt slightly disappointed.

A couple of hours later, as she was washing up out in the back kitchen, Greg walked in and placed his hand on her shoulder. The human touch was lovely. The tingle occurred.

Evie turned around. 'Hey.'

'Hey! All good?'

'Yep, not quite as manic as Christmas Day, but still fun.'

'Did the man come in who you were talking on Christmas Day? What's his name anyway?'

'Yves – and no, he didn't.'

'*Bonjour monsieur.*' Greg put on a French accent. 'I haven't met him before as I would have definitely recognised that name. I don't even remember an Yves on Christmas Day, but let's face it, it was madness the whole of that day here.'

'That's odd. He was definitely here, I served him lunch.'

They finished washing down the surfaces and

Greg took off his apron.

'Right, we're all done if you want to head off, Evie.'

'How about you?'

'Oh me – I am the man who never sleeps. I'm double shifting again.'

'Do you want me to stay?'

'No, no – you go. I don't expect it to be too busy later and I've got three others doing the late shift. It was just lunchtime I was short.' He cleared his throat. 'And . . . Evie?'

'Yes?'

'Oh, it doesn't matter.' Evie could see the colour of his cheeks matching the tint of his heart-shaped birthmark.

'Go on.'

'Would you mind awfully coming in to help again tomorrow?'

'No need to get embarrassed asking me that. Of course I can. Oh, no wait, I'm meeting Yves tomorrow at two and I don't have his number – if he has a mobile, which I doubt.'

'Oh, OK. No worries. Have a good afternoon, won't you, and I'll be in touch.'

'You'd better be.' Evie grinned. 'I haven't done enough to feel even a little bit self-righteous yet.'

CHAPTER EIGHT

Creativity

It was a cold, crisp December day and the Thames was awash with pleasure boats, whipping past in the glistening waters. Evie walked along the South Bank with a spring in her step. Her friendship with Greg might not be one of a sexual kind, but it was a relationship of sorts. And, it made her heart happy to know that she would be welcomed at the Homeless Centre anytime.

She had never been to Shakespeare's Globe and loved anything that was steeped in history. *(Shakespeare's Globe is a reconstruction of the Globe Theatre, an Elizabethan playhouse in the London Borough of Southwark, on the south bank of the River Thames that was originally built in 1599, destroyed by fire in 1613, rebuilt in 1614, and then demolished in 1644. The modern reconstruction is an academic approximation based on available evidence of the 1599 and 1614 buildings.)*

She was also looking forward to seeing Yves and wondered what he had in store for her today. She was determined to find out how a man of quite significant intelligence had found himself in this position.

She saw him puffing on his pipe, swinging his legs over a wall facing out over the water. He looked like a little lost but bearded boy. He was taking in his surroundings and looked completely at ease. She felt as if she could stand and watch him for hours. His whole demeanour exuded happiness. She thought if she could have half of the peace he felt, she'd be more than all right.

She quietly approached and sat next to him on the wall.

'What's a handsome bearded fella like you doing in a place like this?'

Yves didn't move as he replied without missing a beat: 'Waiting for an amazing woman to unleash her potential.'

'Oh, I'd better move on then. Before I do, here's some baccy for you. My Uncle John left it at our place last Christmas and I kept hold of it for some obscure reason.'

'Thanks, Evie. You are kind. It's lovely here, isn't it?'

'Yes. I haven't actually been here before and the relief of not a tall building to climb in sight is actually rather comforting. Uh – oh, what about

Tate Modern? We're not climbing up that, are we?'

'No, you can relax about that. Didn't I mention we were abseiling across the Globe?'

'Erm. See you later.' She pretended to get up.

'I'm glad you brought your camera,' Yves remarked.

'Why's that? Do you want me to take a photo of you?'

'No!' he said a little too sharply.

'It's fine, I know you don't like your photo being taken and I respect that.'

'I just want to make sure you are still using your creative energy, that's all. I think it's a good release for you.'

'To tell you the truth, Yves, photography would be my dream job.'

'Then why don't you follow your dreams?'

'It's not as easy as that!'

'Was that a little negativity I detected slipping in there, Evie?

'It's hard to make a living out of it unless you are really good, and with rent to pay, bills to cope with, clothes to buy, et cetera, I couldn't justify it.'

'You could, if you really wanted to. Initially, it would probably mean making some changes. You might have to move to a less fancy area than Chelsea. You would most definitely need to share, maybe with more than one person. Luxury items might be few and far between. But if you really want something, Evie, it isn't going to be given to you on a plate.'

'I know you're right – there would be an element of risk.'

'Nobody ever got anywhere without an element of risk. If we look at the way humans are designed to learn, we learn by making mistakes. We learn to walk by falling down. If we never fell down, we would never walk.'

'If you put it like that.' Ruby pulled a bottle of water out of her bag. 'I've got a spare if you'd like one?'

'No, thanks, I'm fine.'

'I won't be offended if you take a drink off of me, you know that.'

'I'm just not thirsty, that's all.'

'Yves?'

'Yes, Evie.'

'Do you mind me asking how you came to become homeless?'

'I will reply to you in the words of the great Bard himself, and then we must walk on, for today is not about me, but you. *You can win life by all means, if you simply avoid two things – comparing and expectation.*'

Evie didn't push the homeless question. It obviously was a difficult discussion and when it came down to it, really none of her business.

They walked slowly along the river, taking in the post-Christmas sights and sounds. Children on their new scooters and bikes, wrapped in brand new scarves. Parents in their bright winter coats. Ladies smelling sweetly of their fragrant gifts. Couples getting weekday drunk in bars as no work tomorrow.

Yves smiled as Evie snapped away, the delight in her face so evident.

'I bet you could create enough for a small exhibition out of those and the homeless shelter ones you took alone. In fact, why don't you speak to Greg about it? I bet the church hall run all sorts of things like that when they are not using the Centre for Christmas-time, and I doubt if the outlay would be much at all.'

'Hmm, yes I didn't think of that. Let me concentrate on you now, I got carried away.'

'No, please continue, it's great to see you so happy. I'm just enjoying the moment and this glorious winter sunshine. We are so lucky, Evie.'

After walking for about a mile along the river, they stopped and sat on a bench. Yves turned and looked at Evie. His eyes were so fluid, his soul so obvious and pure, Evie was drawn to hug him.

'You are amazing, Yves with a Y. I feel such a love for you that I can't explain. It's not a boyfriend love; it's somehow deeper than that. I don't know what's happened to me. I hope we can stay friends forever.

Yves took her hand and told her gently, 'Evie, when we see through our hearts, we recognise that every single one of us is infused with creativity. Divine sparks are embedded in everyone. It's up to us to be courageous, to look and listen deeply, to find the sparks, gather them and release them back into the universe, transformed into something new. Your photography will do that, I know. Please don't waste your talent. Promise me.'

'I promise,' Evie whispered. So overwhelmed by the experience of the day she felt she had barely any breath left in her to speak.

'So tell me,' Yves went on to ask her the customary question: 'if you were to use one word to describe how this afternoon's experiences have made you feel, what would it be?'

She needed no time to think.

'Creative – yes, creative. You're right! With will and determination and a little bit of compromise thrown in, we can achieve anything we want to.'

'Good! That's really good, Evie.'

'Anyway, I'm hungry and I'm not going to take no for an answer this time. Please: dinner on me?'

Yves lit his pipe and shook his head, placed a piece of white card in her hand, closed her fingers around it – and by the time she had read it and lifted her head, he was gone.

This time, the little piece of card had the most

beautiful water-colour painting of a ladybird on one side, and on the other in perfect handwriting was: *Meet me at Winter Wonderland tomorrow night at 7*

CHAPTER NINE

'You look lovely with your hair tied back,' Greg greeted her at the door of the Centre. 'And thanks for coming at such short notice, really appreciate it.'

'I never thought I'd say this, but I actually quite like doing my bit for charity – and seeing you is a bonus, of course.' Boom! Greg's face reddened again and he turned away so Evie didn't notice. 'You've got me until six as I'm off to Winter Wonderland at seven.'

'Ooh, that's fun. Going with anyone special?'

'Well, er . . . yes, Yves actually.'

'Oh, OK. Although I'm not sure I should allow you to date the customers.'

Evie laughed. 'It's hardly dating. I just like his company, that's all.'

'Now, who was it who said *Love is friendship set on fire?*' He winked and walked over to chat to another couple of the volunteers who'd just arrived.

Evie went to the kitchen. So Greg had gone red

again even though he thought she hadn't noticed; he was questioning who she was going out with, maybe she'd even detected a slight bit of jealousy. Maybe it wasn't love's young dream with young Shell, after all.

She poured a sack of potatoes into the sink and began peeling them. Singing along to 'Do They Know It's Christmas' she felt happy. She not only felt happy, she realised she hadn't had one negative thought all day. She must ask Greg about the photo exhibition too. Strike whilst the iron was hot. She was on a mission now. She might have to go back to the rat race for a short while and save up, but all the time she could be working on her dream of building up her portfolio and becoming a fulltime photographer.

She wiped her hands on her apron and went and found Greg in the back office. He was on the phone and gestured her to sit down.

'That's brilliant, Shell, well done. Yeah. Yeah. I know you do. It'll be fine. Yep, yep, all go here as usual. Anyway, I've gotta go. Love you and talk New Year's Eve, Bye, darling. Take care.'

He smiled at Evie. 'Shell,' he said unnecessarily.

'Ah, right. She OK?'

'Yes, she's fine. She misses me.'

'I bet she does.' Ah, get off the *girlfriend small talk and let's talk photography*, Evie's inner voice screamed.

'I am in the middle of a very important spud-peeling mission, but I have a quick question.'

Greg stood up. 'Let me come round this to your side of the desk. I feel as if I'm interviewing you, or I'm your boss.'

'Take a letter, Miss Jones, and all that.' Evie giggled, and as her head shook, the hair-band holding back her blonde curls fell to the floor. They both reached to get it and on doing so bumped heads.

'I'm sorry,' Evie said, despite the pain.

'Don't be.' Greg said huskily. 'You look so beautiful.' And, then, without warning, he grabbed Evie round the waist and gave her the sexiest, most passionate and arousing kiss she had ever experienced in her life.

'Shit, it's me who should be sorry now,' he gasped when he drew up for air.

'Yes, you bloody should be.' Evie had fire in her eyes as well as in her heart. 'You have a girlfriend and I have just been cheated on! I know how it feels and I'm sure as hell not going to put somebody through the same hurt as me.'

With that, she ripped off her apron, threw it to the ground and stormed out of the church hall.

By the time she had reached Bea, she had calmed down slightly but not enough not to order a large Bristol Cream blue bottle sherry – with ice – and down it in one.

'What a cock,' she ranted.

'But you fancy him, Evie! In fact, it's what you said you'd quite like to happen. If it had been me, my skirt would have been hitched up and we'd still be at it over that desk.'

'Well thankfully I'm not you, am I?'

'Come on, don't tell me a little bit of you wanted to do just that.'

Evie couldn't contain a wry smile. 'Oh, fuck it, I wish sometimes I could be more like you.' Her phone buzzed. 'He's calling – look.'

'Well, speak to him then.'

'No way.'

Bea sighed. 'Look, if he likes you that much – which he so obviously does – then maybe he will finish with Shell. Would you see him then?'

'I'm not sure – I guess so, but it all seems a bit too soon if he does. They seemed so close on Christmas Day. She ran in and wrapped her legs around him – it was really sweet.'

'But that is all you saw.'

'It was enough to feel the love, all right? Anyway, let's get another drink, and by the way, thanks for coming over here. I'm meeting Yves in a couple of hours, so it's saved me coming all the way back to Chelsea then into town again.' Her phone bleeped. 'He's texted now,' she sighed.

'What's he saying?'

'We need to talk.'

'So talk to the man! Sometimes, Evie!'

'I'm turning my phone off, tomorrow is New Year's Eve, we are going to the Heart and Flowers to party hard and kiss random strangers. I am done with complication and men who are cheaters.'

'I will drink to that, dear friend. To kissing random strangers! Bottoms up!'

CHAPTER TEN

Hope

'I am SO sorry I am late and even sorrier I'm a little tipsy. I'd better not go on any rides now.' Evie greeted Yves with a sherry-laden kiss on the cheeks. 'I got you some peanuts.'

'Evie, you know I think this is commercial rubbish and I don't bring you anywhere to spend money. But thanks for the peanuts, that's sweet of you.'

'Ooh, hark at you.'

'And drinking isn't the answer to shielding pain, you know.'

'How do you know I'm in pain?'

'I can just feel it, that's all. What's happened?'

Just then, a screaming child ran into Evie, sending her handbag flying. Children were everywhere, running between rides and stalls, screaming with both delight and protest.

Yves reached down, picked her bag up, took her hand and led her out of the kerfuffle, to a quiet bench near the opening of Hyde Park. *(Hyde Park is one of the Royal Parks of London, and is famous for its Speakers' Corner. The park has become a traditional location for mass demonstrations. The Chartists, the Reform League, the Suffragettes and the Stop the War Coalition have all held protests in there.)*

Once they were sat down, Evie spilled her tale of woe.

'Greg kissed me. It felt so right – but he has a girlfriend and I don't cheat.'

'Well done you for standing up for what you believe in.'

'But I do really like him,' Evie added wistfully, 'and could actually see myself with him and what if I never meet anyone I fancy and it's too late for me to have a family and I end up all alone and . . .'

'And breathe, Evie . . . just breathe. If only to extinguish all those negatives that just came flying out of your mouth. Now what did I say to you the night I met you? There is always a solution. Have you ever read *The Prophet* by Kahlil Gibran?'

She shook her head.

'Well, I think maybe you should. He has a very interesting take on life and death and everything in between. In fact, what he says about children is a must read.' Yves began to recite.

Your children are not your children.
They are the sons and daughters of Life's

longing for itself.
They come through you but not from you,
And though they are with you, yet they belong not to you.

'They are never truly yours, you see, Evie. And equally, all those poor ladies who can't have children, who have tried and suffered many losses, their little babies' souls just weren't ready for this world yet. When your time is right, you will have your babies, or not. For I truly believe that our lives are written before they even start.'

'Yves, every time I see you, I am in awe of you and what you tell me. However, that still doesn't alter the fact that I am in lust with a man who has a girlfriend.'

'Just talk to him. Communication is key in any sort of relationship, be it business or personal.' He stood up. 'Anyway, you were late and I have to go. I'm sorry.'

'Come and have another little drink with me.' But Evie's flirting tactics were wasted on her scruffy friend.

'No. But, in your slightly drunken state, if you were to use one word to describe to me how tonight's brief experiences have made you feel – what would it be?'

'Hopeful. Hopeful that I will be able to have beautiful babies. Yes, beautiful babies with Greg.

Oh, I don't even know his surname either, that's strange. All these men floating around me and I don't know their names.'

'How are you getting home, Evie?'

'It's fine, Bea is still in the bar, she is waiting for me and we'll get a taxi together.'

'Good.' He placed a piece of white card in her hand, closed her fingers around it, turned, walked away – and had vanished into the crowd.

The piece of card had the most beautiful watercolour painting of a cherub on one side and on the other in perfect handwriting was:

Meet me at the lake in St James Park at midday on New Year's Eve

CHAPTER ELEVEN

Love

'My head hurts,' Bea boomed out on loudspeaker mode as Evie made herself some fresh coffee.

'Me too. I think a little disco kip may be required before we hit the Heart and Flowers later. Oh shit!'

'What's the matter?'

'I'm meeting Yves in St James Park at midday.'

'Can't you rearrange?'

'No. He doesn't have a phone – he's homeless, remember.'

'Oh yes, I keep forgetting. Evie, my young friend, you spend more time with him than anyone: are you sure you haven't got a thing for his dirty bits?'

'Bea, stop now. It's fine. I'll have a little siesta on my return. I'm going to drive over there so I don't have to wait for public transport. It's bloody freezing and the forecast said it may snow later.'

'Well, good job we can walk to the pub then.

So did you message Birthmark Boy then?'

'Don't be rude, Bea. But yes, I said I'd meet him on New Year's Day at the pub opposite the Centre.'

'That's good. He's obviously not seeing lover girl tonight then?'

'No. I knew that already as I had overheard a phone conversation.'

'It can't be that serious in that case?'

'I'll know tomorrow, won't I? She is training to be a doctor though. It's her last year, so she's probably working.'

'I didn't think of that. Right – what time shall we say later?'

'How about we meet at yours for a little aperitif at around seven?'

'Perfect. And I think Evie should now go get jiggy with Christmas Yvie behind the Pagoda in the park.'

'Ha, very funny. Now clear off and I'll see you later. What are you wearing, by the way?'

'The black dress with the fifties flared skirt I wore to the office party. No one will be there to know I've worn it twice.'

'Great to have that luxury, you tart. See you.'

'I didn't realise the lake at St James's Park was this

bloody big.' Evie said under her breath, worried that she'd miss Yves. Just as she did so she saw a familiar figure walking towards her. He was wearing his overcoat and a big red scarf. *(St. James's Park is the oldest of the Royal Parks of London. It lies at the southernmost tip of the St James's area, which was named after a leper hospital dedicated to St James the Less.)*

'That was a coincidence, seeing you here,' Evie laughed. 'I thought I wouldn't be able to find you.'

Yves smiled knowingly.

'Here, I've even wrapped it for you.' Evie handed him an oblong package.

'Oh Evie, I don't want gifts from you.'

'It's fine, it cost me nothing. Let's sit on this bench, but not for long, it's bloody freezing.'

Yves unwrapped the package, picked up Evie's hand and kissed it.

'It's beautiful,' he said. 'See, I told you you could do it. People would pay good money for a photograph like that.' A black and white image of the Thames and pleasure boats looked back at him. 'I love it. Thank you.'

'I've even brought along my camera today. No moment will ever be missed,' she told him, beaming.

'That's the spirit. You're like a new woman already.' He changed the subject. 'So have you spoken to Greg?'

'I am speaking to him tomorrow.'

'Oh, OK. Why wait?'

'I'm out tonight with Bea for New Year's Eve and I know it's going to be a difficult conversation. And . . .'

'And what?'

'I'm worried that if I see him on New Year's Eve, I might get carried away by the occasion and do or say something I wouldn't be proud of.'

'Evie, you are a good woman. Love will win. It always does. So, if it's written, he will come to you.'

'I want to have his babies.'

'And now you've said that to me, I very much expect you will.'

'What do you mean?'

'Have you heard of the Law of Attraction, Evie?'

'No, what is it?'

'The Law of Attraction is the name given to the belief that "like attracts like" and that by focusing on positive or negative thoughts, one can bring about positive or negative results. The belief is based upon the idea that people and their thoughts are both made from pure energy, therefore like energy attracts like energy.'

'Ooh, hence you always telling me to think positive thoughts!'

'Well, it can't harm the soul in any way whatsoever, can it?'

'Yves – are you OK?'

'Of course I am. But I won't be seeing you again, Evie.'

'Don't be silly. Once I've made it up with Greg I'll be at the Centre loads. You can come and have a chat and we can do things that don't cost money together.'

'No. I've got to go away now. But never worry about me. I am truly happy and content and at complete peace, I promise you.' Evie was sure she could see real tears in his beautiful green eyes.

'Would it be foolish to say "I love you" after just a few days?' she said, nearly in tears herself. 'Not romantically – oh, you know what I mean.'

'It would not be at all foolish. There are many aspects of love. And ultimately, love will engulf *you* with calm and at peace. When I am not by your side, always remember something else Kahlil Gibran said – *Yesterday is but today's memory, and tomorrow is today's dream.*'

'He sure came out with some corkers, didn't he, that Gibran fellow?'

Evie was trying her hardest not to cry, but couldn't stop one lone tear falling slowly down her cheek.

'Please don't cry, sweet Evie with an E. You really don't need to, because I know now that one day I will see you again.' Yves gently wiped the tear away with his thumb. 'I have one more card for you too.'

As he was rooting around in his coat she sneakily took a photo of him on the small camera she carried in her pocket. She couldn't have him leave her without having some sort of memory of his beautiful, intelligent and knowing face.

'Here.' He bent her fingers around the card and before she even had time to thank him, he was gone.

CHAPTER TWELVE

It was 11.30 p.m. and the Heart and Flowers was heaving. The band were having a quick break and one of the barmaids was checking that the big screen was working, ready for the countdown and firework display.

Bea pushed her way to the bar, instructing Evie to grab a place against one of the high tables in the middle of the makeshift dance floor.

She returned with an ice-bucket and two flutes.

'You really didn't have to get champagne, Bea.'

'Oh, yes I did. If I can't treat my old mucker to a bottle of bubbles tonight of all nights, then when can I? Cheers!'

'Cheers! Right, well, it's my duty then to check out if there are any random strangers for us to kiss.'

'Will I do?' The interloper was around six foot, in his early forties, had blue eyes with crinkly lines around them, a wide-mouthed smile, cropped dark hair and a small heart-shaped birthmark on his cheek.

'What the . . .'

Greg handed her a beautiful bunch of red roses. 'Well, I have the heart already,' he pointed to his birthmark, 'so these just made sense.'

'But I said we would talk tomorrow and I really don't understand.'

The band started up again.

'I can't hear you!' Greg shouted. 'Come on, let's go outside.'

Evie looked to Bea who nodded frantically. She was already pouring a floppy-fringed young guy a glass of fizz, so Evie knew she wouldn't miss her too much.

They managed to find a seat amongst the smokers. An outdoor heater was on but Greg removed his coat anyway and put it around Evie gently.

'What are you doing here, Greg?' Evie was curt.

'You invited me.' He looked perplexed.

'No. I said we'd talk tomorrow.'

'Look, I'm not sure who is going mad here – you or me?'

He put a white card in her hand. On one side was a beautiful water colour of a hummingbird; on the other the words *Greg, meet me in the Heart and Flowers before midnight. Evie x*

'It had been pushed through the letterbox at the Centre late last night.'

'We've been set up.' Evie smiled.

'Is that such a terrible thing?'

'Well, considering that you and Shell are an item, it is, yes.'

Greg threw his head back and laughed, took a slurp of his beer then laughed again.

'Me and Shell, honestly? Evie. Shell is my sister!'

'What? But? She came flying up to you on Christmas Day and you seemed so close... and—'

'And what? Oh, Evie. She had been at our parents' for the day but promised she'd come and see me and help that night. I'm pretty open-minded but even I would draw the line at incest.' He laughed again.

'So you're single?'

'Yes, with a big fat capital S. I can't believe you didn't pick up the signs of how much I fancy you. You – yes, you. Beautiful, kind, compassionate and talented Evie. With the amazing mop of blonde curls and figure to die for.'

'Aw, really.' Evie felt herself tingling all over. 'I feel the same.'

'You do?'

Evie began to gabble excitedly. 'A million times over. I've never really believed in love at first sight and I was devastated when Shell arrived and that's why I didn't say goodbye and that's when I went outside and met Yves. And, as for Yves, he has taught me so much about life and loving in the space of days – and do you know what? I don't care what I'm going to say next.'

DONG! The first bell of Big Ben rang out from the huge TV in the pub and big flakes of snow began to fall slowly.

'I think I love you!' she cried out.

'Come here, you.'

Greg pulled Evie towards him, wrapped his coat more tightly around her and kissed her with such tenderness that she thought she might actually properly melt.

'And I think I love you back,' he murmured happily.

Bea came running outside with champagne in one hand, toy boy in the other, bawling: 'Happy New Year!' She planted kisses on both Evie and Greg.

'Do you know what, Bea? I really do think it is going to be a very happy one indeed.'

Once the excitement of the New Year's Eve revelry had subsided, Greg and Evie walked hand in hand towards her house.

'There was one thing I never asked you, Greg,' she said shyly.

'Go on.'

'What is your surname?'
'Promise not to laugh.'
'I promise.'
'It's Love.'

EPILOGUE

January 31

What a difference a month makes! Just a few weeks ago Evie was wondering how on earth she would be able to afford the rent. And, now not only did she have an amazing new man, she was moving in with him to his beautiful four-bedroomed home and even more exciting was that he had allocated a room for her to use as a photographic studio. She was obviously going to pay her way once she had got herself up and running but at the moment he said that wasn't necessary, he just wanted her to be happy.

You see Greg was actually very rich, not only in spirit but financially. His IT company had floated on the stock market and made him a tidy sum, hence him working at the Centre. He didn't want to just waste his time on frivolity, he wanted to put something back into society. He had been looking for a partner for years, but most seemed to be after one thing. In Evie, from the minute he had clapped eyes on those blonde bouncy curls and sad, but true eyes, he had seen nothing but good.

Evie walked around the house to check she hadn't missed any of her possessions whilst packing. To be honest most of the big stuff had belonged to Darren and he had taken all of his belongings last weekend. She had even managed to be civil and wish him a happy life. She had let him go with love and it had actually felt good. Since meeting Greg, she had realised just how wrong her and Darren were as a couple, so it hadn't been that hard to do really.

She had also realised since meeting Yves that yes material possessions were nice to have, but that was it. They were throw aways that was all. In the big scheme of things they didn't matter at all.

She looked out to the garden and noticed a Robin fly down to the bird table. It made her think of the Hummingbird card that Yves had so obviously put through the Centre door. She missed him. He had had such a strong impact on her life in such a short time. In fact, he had changed her life for the better forever.

She gasped as she suddenly realised she hadn't opened the card that he had given her in an envelope the day she last saw him.

She found the coat that she had been wearing that day in a pile of clothes that were ready to throw in the car and pulled out the envelope. The compact camera she had been carrying that day was there also.

The card: on one side a beautiful water colour of a butterfly and on the other the word LOVE.

Aw. Love was definitely all around her now. In fact it was only a matter of time she thought before she would actually be Mrs Evie Love. Especially as Greg had already agreed that they could try for a baby.

Evie then sat down on the bed and felt *the tingle* engulf her. She could feel Yves all around her as words flew into her mind. Peace, Freedom, Hope, Creativity and Love and then the images – the dove, the eagle, the cherub, the ladybird, the hummingbird and finally the butterfly.

Yves was right, nothing in life was a coincidence. She would look up what all the perfectly painted images symbolised, but not today.

Reaching for the camera, she took a deep breath and tentatively scrolled to the last photo she had taken of Yves in St James's Park.

And, there staring right back at her was not the face of her wonderful, spiritual, bearded companion, but the face of her beautiful, loving and creative mother.

xXx

If you enjoyed this story of hope and happiness it would be lovely if you could pop a review up on Amazon/Goodreads for me.

Now go follow YOUR dreams... LOVE Nicola X